D1222577

NEARLY FEARLESS

MONKEY PIRATES

ESCAPE FROM HAUNTED TREASURE ISLAND

A 4D BOOK

BY MICHAEL ANTHONY STEELE

ILLUSTRATED BY PAULINE REEVES

PICTURE WINDOW BOOKS
a capstone imprint

Nearly Fearless Monkey Pirates is published by Stone Arch Books,
A Capstone Imprint
1710 Roe Crest Drive
North Mankato, Minnesota 56003
www.capstonepub.com

Cataloging-in-Publication Data is available on the Library of Congress website.
ISBN: 978-1-5158-2678-1 (library binding)
ISBN: 978-1-5158-2686-6 (paperback)
ISBN: 978-1-5158-2690-3 (eBook PDF)

Summary: The Nearly Fearless Monkey Pirates sail to a secret treasure island
where they come face-to-face with pirate ghosts! Will they escape, or will
they walk the haunted plank?

Designer: Ted Williams

Design elements:
Shutterstock: Angeliki Vel, MAD SNAIL, nazlisart

Printed and bound in the USA
PA021

Download the Capstone app!

- Ask an adult to download the Capstone 4D app.

- Scan the cover and stars inside the book for additional content.

When you scan a spread, you'll find
fun extra stuff to go with this book!
You can also find these things
on the web at www.capstone4D.com
using the password: haunted.26781

TABLE OF CONTENTS

CHAPTER 1
MONKEY PIRATE PRACTICE
PAGE 7

CHAPTER 2
FLYING COCONUTS
PAGE 16

CHAPTER 3
THE HAUNTED HUNT
PAGE 24

CHAPTER 4
INTO THE VOLCANO
PAGE 31

CHAPTER 5
MR. PICKLES AND THE MAP
PAGE 35

MEET THE CREW

CAPTAIN BANANA BEARD

Captain Banana Beard is the almost brave leader of the monkey pirates. Banana Beard often puts his search for treasure before the safety of his crew. But he's always sure to give credit where credit is due!

FIRST MATE FEZ

Wearing a red fez hat (wonder how he got his name?), Fez is in charge of the ship's charts and books. He tries to keep Captain Banana Beard's plans from getting too crazy, but that's a nearly impossible job for any monkey!

BANANA JUICE

BANANAS

CREWMAN MR. PICKLES

Mr. Pickles is the lowest on the chain of command, but he's still excited to be the best pirate he can be. With every job he does, Mr. Pickles is one step closer to being a great pirate captain, just like his hero, Captain Banana Beard.

QUARTERMASTER FOSSEY

Fossey keeps track of the ship's goods and treasure. She's in charge of all the gear and knows the supplies down to the last banana. And if the adventure calls for a certain tool that the ship doesn't have, Fossey can build it in record time.

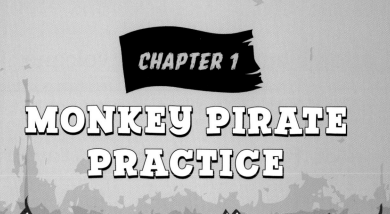

CHAPTER 1

MONKEY PIRATE PRACTICE

"When I'm a monkey pirate captain," Mr. Pickles said to himself, "I'll have to draw treasure maps all the time."

The young monkey drew with crayons behind two banana barrels. He made his very own treasure map.

The map showed one large island with two smaller ones.

A large banana-shaped volcano poked out of the big island.

Mr. Pickles used a black crayon to add three birds flying high in the sky. Then he drew an X with a red crayon on the large island.

"X marks the spot," Mr. Pickles said. "That's where I would bury my treasure."

"Mr. Pickles!" Fossey called. "Where are you?"

"Coming!" replied Mr. Pickles. He rolled up the map and shoved it inside an empty bottle.

Fossey leaned over the banana barrels. Mr. Pickles hid the bottle behind his back.

"There you are," Fossey said. "The captain needs a volunteer."

"Aye-aye," said Mr. Pickles. That was monkey pirate talk for *yes*. He stood and saw the rest of the crew gathered around him. Mr. Pickles saluted the captain.

CLINK! He hit his head with the bottle.

"Ouch," said Mr. Pickles.

"What did ye find, lad?" asked the captain. He snatched up the bottle.

"Well, sir . . . ," Mr. Pickles began.

"Ooh, a message in a bottle," the captain interrupted.

He removed the cork and unrolled the drawing. His eyes widened. "No, it's a treasure map!" He slapped Mr. Pickles on the back. "Well done, lad!"

Fez leaned closer. "It's drawn with crayons."

"So? Treasure maps come in all shapes and sizes," said the captain. "Did I ever tell you about the time I made a treasure map out of a banana peel?"

"Aye-aye, Captain," everyone replied.

Captain Banana Beard pointed to the birds on the map.

"Now, see these here?"
he asked.

"Those squiggly lines?"
asked Fossey.

"Aye," replied the captain.
"Those birds be blackleberry
sap-suckers."

"Begging the captain's pardon,"
said Mr. Pickles.

"Do be quiet, Mr. Pickles," the
captain growled. "That's an order."

Mr. Pickles opened his mouth
to reply. Then he closed it. He
couldn't disobey the captain's
orders.

Banana Beard continued.
"Now, the blackleberry sap-sucker
flies east this time of year. So
prepare to set sail!" The captain
grinned. "East!"

CHAPTER 2
FLYING COCONUTS

"Land ho!" Fossey shouted. That was monkey pirate talk for *I see some land.*

Mr. Pickles couldn't believe his ears. He joined everyone at the front of the ship.

A *real* island poked out of the sea. It had two smaller ones nearby. The big one even had a banana-shaped volcano. They looked just like the islands he had drawn.

"What did I say, mateys?" asked
the captain. "There she be. Our
treasure island!"

The monkey pirates took a smaller boat to shore. Then they entered a thick jungle. Captain Banana Beard led the way. He held the treasure map open.

"This way, mateys," he said. "We'll have that treasure in no time!"

Fez and Fossey marched behind him. Mr. Pickles brought up the rear. He carried several shovels.

The jungle was dark and spooky. Mr. Pickles felt as if someone or something was watching his every move.

"This is one creepy island," Fossey whispered.

"You said it," Fez agreed. "I hope it's not far to the—ouch!" A coconut flew off the ground and hit him.

"What's wrong?" asked Fossey.

Fez rubbed his face. "A coconut just hit my chin."

"How did a falling coconut hit your chin?" she asked.

"It didn't fall," replied Fez. "It flew up."

Fossey shook her head. "Coconuts fall down, not—"

She stopped in the middle of
her sentence as coconuts flew off
the ground around them. The
monkey pirates ducked and
dodged them.

"What's going on?" asked Fez.

Mr. Pickles couldn't take it anymore. He dropped the tools and ran to the front of the line. He tugged on the captain's coat.

"What is it, Mr. Pickles?" asked Banana Beard.

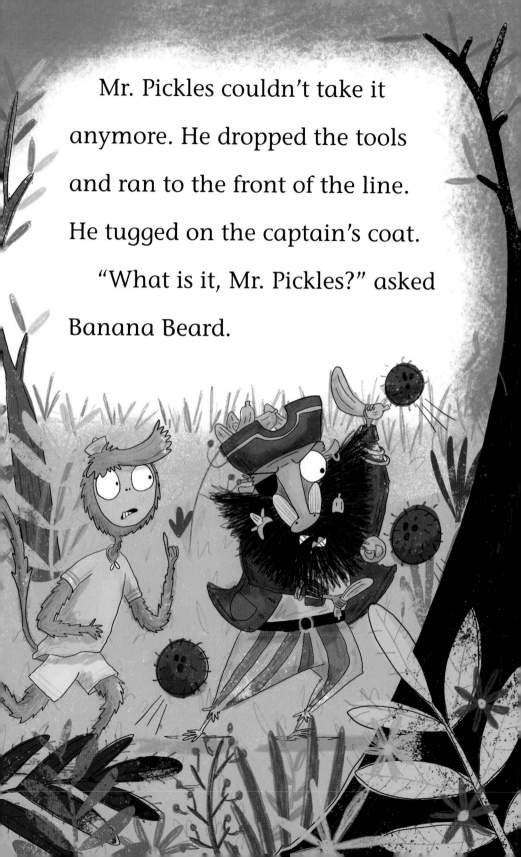

Mr. Pickles pointed at himself and then at the map.

The captain rolled his eyes. "Yes, I know. You found the map. I told you 'well done, lad,' didn't I?"

Mr. Pickles nodded and pointed at the map again.

"Just yo-ho-hold that thought," said the captain. He squinted his eyes. "I must first bow to his majesty, the monkey pirate king, Captain Shaggypants the Third."

The captain bowed to the large monkey pirate standing in the jungle ahead of them.

That is, he bowed to the large *glowing* monkey pirate.

"Uh . . . begging the captain's pardon," said Fez, "but Captain Shaggypants . . . has been dead for one hundred years."

"That means that he's . . . he's . . . ," began Fossey.

"A ghost!" finished Fez.

"Who dares set foot on me haunted island?" asked the ghost of Captain Shaggypants.

Banana Beard bowed again. "'Tis I. Captain . . . RUN!" He turned and dashed past the others. Fez, Fossey, and Mr. Pickles hurried after him.

Captain Shaggypants scratched his head.

"Captain Run, eh?" he said. "A fitting name. He does run quite well." He pointed at the fleeing monkey pirates. "After them!"

Three more ghost monkey pirates appeared. They glowed brightly as they floated through the jungle.

Fez caught up to Banana Beard. "What are your orders, Captain?"

"First, we lose the ghosts," the captain replied. "Then we circle back around and get me treasure."

Mr. Pickles tugged at Captain Banana Beard's coat again.

"Not now, Mr. Pickles," said the captain. "You sure are a pest this adventure."

Fossey ducked as a coconut whizzed past her head. "I don't think we can lose them, Captain." She pointed to the trees. "Look!"

The ghost monkey pirates floated above them, flinging coconuts their way.

"Two can play that game," said the captain. "Fez, climb up and fetch me some coconuts."

Fez gulped. "Aye, Captain."

He sprung from the ground and grabbed a vine. He raced up it and leaped out for another.

Unfortunately, the vine grabbed him. It snaked around his body and held him tight.

The captain skidded to a halt. "Yo-ho-holy-moly!" he cried.

Suddenly vines came to life all around them! They wrapped themselves around each of the Nearly Fearless Monkey Pirates. The vines held the crew high above the jungle floor.

"Let me down!"
Banana Beard
demanded. "I'll
not be a monkey
pirate piñata!"

The ghost of Captain
Shaggypants floated forward.
He drew his long sword. "Nowhere
to run, Captain Run," he said.

"It's actually Captain Banana
Beard," Fossey corrected.

"Oh, really? Well . . . good," said Shaggypants. "That is a bit more fitting for a monkey pirate, for certain." He looked over his shoulder. "First Mate Topper!"

"Aye, Captain," said one of the ghost monkey pirates. He wore a ragged top hat.

"Throw them into the volcano!" ordered Shaggypants. "No one comes to me island and lives to tell the tale!"

The ghost monkey pirates drew their swords. Mr. Pickles squeezed his eyes shut as they floated closer.

WHAK! WHAK! WHAK-WHAK!

The ghosts sliced through the vines holding up the monkey pirates. The prisoners fell to the jungle floor. **THUD!** They were still wrapped tightly with thinner vines.

"Ouch," said Captain Banana Beard. "That hurt a lot. So . . . I think we've learned our lesson. Haven't we, mateys?"

"Oh, yes," said Fez.

"You bet," agreed Fossey.

Mr. Pickles nodded.

"So we'll just be on our way now," said Banana Beard.

Shaggypants grinned. "I think not," he said.

The ghost pirates picked up each of the monkey pirates. They floated up over the treetops, drifting higher and higher.

The ghost pirates were nearing the top of the smoking volcano. Mr. Pickles could keep quiet no longer. "Captain!" he shouted. "Permission to speak, sir?"

"You just spoke," replied the captain. "I ordered you to be quiet!"

"But I was asking permission, sir," said Mr. Pickles.

"You spoke again!" said Captain Banana Beard. "This isn't like you at all, lad. Disobeying orders."

"Might as well let him speak," said Captain Shaggypants. "For they be his last words."

Just then, the ghost of Captain Shaggypants grabbed Mr. Pickles. He held him over the mouth of the volcano. Mr. Pickles trembled with fear.

CHAPTER 5

MR. PICKLES AND THE MAP

"It's all my fault!" shouted
Mr. Pickles.

"What?" asked the ghost of
Captain Shaggypants.

Captain Banana Beard nodded.
"It's true. There's no need to throw
all of us in. He's the one who
found the map!"

Shaggypants squinted. "What
map?" he asked.

"This one right here." The captain squirmed an arm free. He reached into his beard and pulled out . . .

"A banana?" Shaggypants asked. "Who makes maps out of bananas?" He turned to Topper. "What are monkey pirates becoming these days?"

"I think bananas make fine maps," Banana Beard mumbled to himself. He tossed the banana and reached in again. This time he pulled out the map.

Shaggypants snatched up the map. He unrolled it and looked it over. "Where did you find this?"

"I . . ." Mr. Pickles glanced around nervously. "I drew it."

"You what?!" asked Banana Beard, Fez, and Fossey.

"I tried to tell you, Captain," Mr. Pickles explained.

"Hmm . . ." Captain Shaggypants studied it some more. "A fine job."

"Really?" asked Mr. Pickles.

"Really?" asked Fez and Fossey.

"I especially like the blackleberry sap-suckers at the top here," the ghost captain added. "This is top notch. You'll make a fine monkey pirate captain someday."

"I will?" asked Mr. Pickles.

"He will?" asked Banana Beard.

The ghost captain crumpled up the map. "New orders. Throw the map into the volcano and let everyone else go."

The ghosts carried the monkey pirates back to the jungle. The vines around them loosened. They were free.

"Thank you, Your Majesty," said
Banana Beard.

Shaggypants held up a finger.
"But you must promise to leave
and never return."

Banana Beard nodded. "Oh, yes. But about the treasure," the captain added. "I don't suppose a bunch of ghosts really need gold, do you?"

"Go!" roared the ghost.

Captain Banana Beard led the way as the monkey pirates ran back to the ship.

"Just so you know, Mr. Pickles," the captain said as he ran, "I'll be taking away your crayons from now on."

Mr. Pickle sighed. "Aye-aye, Captain."

ABOUT THE AUTHOR

Michael Anthony Steele has been in the entertainment industry for more than twenty years. He has worked in several capacities of film and television production from props and special effects all the way up to writing and directing. For many years, Mr. Steele has written exclusively for family entertainment. For television and video, he wrote for shows including *WISHBONE*, *Barney & Friends*, and *Boz, The Green Bear Next Door*. He has authored more than one hundred books for various characters and brands including *Batman*, *Green Lantern*, *LEGO City*, *Spider-Man*, *The Hardy Boys*, *Garfield*, and *Night at the Museum*.

ABOUT THE ILLUSTRATOR

Pauline Reeves lives by the sea in southwest England, with her husband, two children, and dog Jenson. She has loved drawing and creating since she was a child. Following her passion, Ms. Reeves graduated from Plymouth College of Art with a degree in illustration, and she specializes in children's literature. She takes inspiration from the funny and endearing things animals and people do every day. Ms. Reeves works both digitally and with traditional materials to create quirky illustrations with humor and charm.

GLOSSARY

crumple (KRUMP-uhl)—to crush something into wrinkles and folds

disobey (dis-oh-BAY)—to go against the rules

dodge (DOJ)—to avoid something by moving quickly

permission (pur-MISH-uhn)—the OK to do something

piñata (pin-YAH-tah)—a decorated container filled with candy that is hung up at parties or celebrations and hit with a stick by children until it is broken and the candy inside falls out

ragged (RAG-id)—old, torn, worn out

volunteer (vol-uhn-TIHR)—to offer to do something without pay

1. How would the story have been different if Captain Banana Beard had listened to Mr. Pickles?

2. Captain Shaggypants tells Mr. Pickles that he will make a "fine monkey pirate captain someday." Do you agree? Why or why not?

FOR YOUR PIRATE LOG

1. Captain Banana Beard isn't always a great leader. Make a list of qualities that you think make someone a good leader.

2. Captain Shaggypants' island is haunted by magic coconuts and attacking vines. What other spooky and special things may be lurking on the island? Use your imagination and write a paragraph that describes your ideas.

3. Draw a pirate map of your school. Decide where you would bury the treasure (and what the treasure would be). Now give it to a friend and see if they can read it!

THE SHIP DOESN'T STOP HERE!

Discover more at www.capstonekids.com

- VIDEOS & CONTESTS
- GAMES & PUZZLES
- FRIENDS & FAVORITES
- AUTHORS & ILLUSTRATORS

Find cool websites and more books like this one at **www.facthound.com**.

Just type in the Book ID: 9781515826781 and you're ready to go!